Ruthie
and the (Not So)
Very Busy Day

Laura Rankin

BLOOMSBURY

NEW YORK LONDON NEW DELHI SYDNEY

First published in the United States of America in May 2014
by Bloomsbury Children's Books
www.bloomsbury.com

For information about permission to reproduce selections from this book, write to
Permissions, Bloomsbury Children's Books, 1385 Broadway, New York, New York 10018
Bloomsbury books may be purchased for business or promotional use. For information on bulk
purchases please contact Macmillan Corporate and Premium Sales Department at
specialmarkets@macmillan.com

Library of Congress Cataloging-in-Publication Data
Rankin, Laura, author, illustrator.
Ruthie and the (not so) very busy day / by Laura Rankin ; illustrated by Laura Rankin.
pages   cm
Summary: Ruthie loves to spend Saturday with her parents, but will interruptions spoil her favorite day?
ISBN 978-1-59990-052-0 (hardcover) · ISBN 978-1-61963-162-5 (reinforced)
ISBN 978-1-61963-211-0 (e-book) · ISBN 978-1-61963-212-7 (e-PDF)
[1. Family life—Fiction. 2. Parent and child—Fiction.] I. Title.
PZ7.R16825Rv 2014   [E]—dc23   2013034315

Art created with color pencil and watercolor on watercolor paper
Typeset in Buccardi
Book design by Yelena Safronova and Donna Mark

Printed in China by C&C Offset Printing Co., Ltd., Shenzhen, Guangdong
2 4 6 8 10 9 7 5 3 1 (hardcover)
2 4 6 8 10 9 7 5 3 1 (reinforced)

All papers used by Bloomsbury Publishing, Inc., are natural, recyclable products
made from wood grown in well-managed forests. The manufacturing processes
conform to the environmental regulations of the country of origin.

For families and "the best laid plans" . . .

Saturday!

No school, no homework, no practices—just a fun, don't-have-to-go-anywhere day with Momma and Papa!

Ruthie had *Big Plans*.

First, they'd have
blueberry pancakes . . .

then she'd watch her
favorite cartoon . . .

then plant flowers with
Papa . . .

and bake cookies
with Momma.
It would be the
Best Kind of Day!

Ruthie was getting out ingredients when Papa rushed through the kitchen.

"'Morning, Papa. Ready for blueberry pancakes?" asked Ruthie.

"Sorry, Ruthie," said Papa. "Change of plans . . . Gramma's basement is flooded!"

Ruthie was going to ask about planting flowers,
but Papa was already bicycling away.

Just then, Momma hurried in. "I forgot today is your cousin Buster's birthday party," she said.

"I don't want to go to Buster's birthday party," said Ruthie. "He's mean to me."

"But Aunt Dorothy would miss us if we weren't there," said Momma.

"Aren't we having blueberry pancakes?" asked Ruthie.

"There's no time," said Momma. "We have to go get a present."

Ruthie's Big Plans were getting smaller every minute.
She ate four bites of cold cereal, then went upstairs
to change.

"If we *have* to go to the party, *I want to wear my polka-dot dress*," said Ruthie.

"Fine," said Momma. "But I'll need to wash it."

The day was looking brighter when Ruthie and Momma drove to the toy store, found the perfect present for Buster, and finished their shopping in record time.

But on the drive home, traffic was bumper-to-bumper.
"I'm missing my show!" cried Ruthie. She kicked the
back of the seat.
"Please stop that," said Momma.

Back home, Ruthie's favorite cartoon was just ending.

"Ruthie," said Momma, "please make Buster a card."

"I don't want to," said Ruthie.

"But you make such beautiful cards, sweetie," said Momma.

So Ruthie quickly drew a picture and wrote:

"Maybe we'll forget about a card," said Momma.

"It's not fair!" Ruthie cried. "We were going to eat pancakes and watch my show and bake cookies. This is not the day I wanted!"

"It's not exactly the day I wanted either," said Momma.

From the laundry room came a loud *buzzzzzzzzzzzzz!*
Then a *clunk!*

Bang! Bang! CLUNK!

Ruthie's polka-dot dress was one big, soggy lump.

"You'll have to wear something else to the party,"
said Momma.

But Ruthie didn't want to wear something else.

This was not a no-school, no-homework, no-practices, don't-have-to-go-anywhere kind of day with Momma and Papa.

It was the Worst Kind of Day *EVER*!

Ruthie stormed out the door.

Stomping down the driveway, she remembered
she couldn't cross the street by herself.
Instead, she scrambled under a bush.

Ruthie's face was
hot. She threw a stone.

She whacked at the grass.

She wished she
could disappear.

After a while she felt the softness of a dandelion. She picked one.

Ruthie's face didn't feel hot anymore.

When she finally peeked out, she saw Momma on the
front steps.

"We both picked dandelions," Ruthie said.

"You know what that means, don't you?" said Momma.

"We both get to make a wish."

Hissssss!

"I don't believe it!" Momma exclaimed, pointing.

Ruthie looked. Their car had a very, very flat tire.

"So, no party after all?" Ruthie asked.

Momma started laughing. Then Ruthie did too.

"I'd better call Aunt Dorothy," said Momma.

"Guess what!" said Ruthie. "There are two eggs that didn't break."

Papa was just coming in the back door. "That sounds like just enough for . . ."

". . . baking cookies!" said Ruthie.

And that was a perfect way to start Ruthie's
Best Kind of Day . . . all over again.